How Do Your Garden Grow?

Monosmith

By Frances Ann Ladd
Illustrated by Jay Johnson

ISBN 0-439-54962-0

12 11 10 9 8 7 6 5 4 3   4 5 6 7 8 9/0

Printed in the U.S.A.
First printing, February 2004

SCHOLASTIC INC.
New York   Toronto   London   Auckland   Sydney
Mexico City   New Delhi   Hong Kong   Buenos Aires

"It is a beautiful day,"
said Funshine Bear.
"What should we do?"

"Let's plant a garden,"
said Cheer Bear.

"Let's make it a
rainbow-colored garden!"
said Bedtime Bear.

"Good idea!"
said Friend Bear.

The Care Bears went
to find their seeds.

"I like pink tulips,"
said Cheer Bear.
"The bulbs are
in my pot."

"I will grow
yellow sunflowers,"
said Funshine Bear.
"The seeds are
in my bucket."

"Can I plant green
four-leaf clovers?"
asked Good Luck Bear.

"Of course!"
said Friend Bear.

"Oh, no!" said Friend Bear.
"My bucket of daisy seeds is gone."
"Here it is," said Good Luck Bear.

"No," said Friend Bear.
"That's Bedtime Bear's
bucket of sweet dreams."

The Care Bears met
at the Cloud Patch.
"What is wrong?"
asked Wish Bear.

"I can't find
my daisy seeds,"
said Friend Bear.

"I wish you could find them,"
said Wish Bear.

"That's okay," said Friend Bear.
"I can help you plant your seeds."

"Let me help you
dig your holes,"
said Friend Bear.

"Thank you,"
said Love-a-lot Bear.

"You look sleepy,"
said Friend Bear.
"I can plant your seeds."

"That is a big help,"
yawned Bedtime Bear.

"May I water that row?"
asked Friend Bear.

"Yes, please,"
said Good Luck Bear.

Soon, the Care Bears were done.
"Thank you for your help,"
Funshine Bear said to Friend Bear.

"We couldn't have done it
without you," said Cheer Bear.
And the Care Bears went to play.

That night, Bedtime Bear
sprinkled sweet dreams
on the garden.

Then he looked at his bucket.
"Uh-oh," said Bedtime Bear.
"This is not my bucket."

Many weeks passed.
The garden grew.
Friend Bear got a big surprise.

"How did my daisies grow?"
asked Friend Bear.
"I wish I knew," said Wish Bear.

"I know," said Friend Bear.
"It was Bedtime Bear.
Our buckets got mixed up."

"He sprinkled daisies
instead of dreams."

"Maybe," said Love-a-lot Bear.
"Or maybe your friendship
helps everything grow!"